The Fangs, Vampire Spy, series

FANGS

VAMPIRE SPY

PROJECT: WOLF WORLD

TOMMY DONBAVAND

WALKER
BOOKS

First published 2014 by Walker Books Ltd
87 Vauxhall Walk, London SE11 5HJ

10 9 8 7 6 5 4 3 2 1

Text © 2014 Tommy Donbavand
Illustrations © 2014 Cartoon Saloon Ltd

The right of Tommy Donbavand to be identified
as author of this work has been asserted by him
in accordance with the Copyright, Designs and
Patents Act 1988

This book has been typeset in Helvetica and Journal

Printed and bound in Great Britain
by Clays Ltd, St Ives plc

British Library Cataloguing in Publication Data:
a catalogue record for this book is available from
the British Library

ISBN 978-1-4063-3162-2

www.walker.co.uk

www.fangsvampirespy.co.uk

For Dad and Barbs

MPI Personnel

Agent Fangs Enigma
World's greatest vampire spy

Agent Puppy Brown
Wily werewolf and Fangs's super sidekick

Phlem
Head of MP1

Miss Bile
Phlem's personal
secretary

**Professor
Hubert Cubit,
aka Cube**
Head of MP1's
technical division

Secret agent and werewolf Puppy Brown
approached the aeroplane's only passenger,
a golem by the name of Clang. "Can I take that
bag for you, sir?" she asked. "You'll be more
comfortable with it in the overhead locker."

The passenger clutched his canvas rucksack
to his chest and shook his head. Puppy sighed.
Still, on the plus side, Clang hadn't seen through
her air-hostess disguise.

She returned to the cockpit and slumped into
the co-pilot's seat. Next to her, flying the specially
chartered plane, was a vampire – Fangs Enigma.
He too was a secret agent. They both worked for

MP1, an organization sworn to protect the world from criminal *monster*minds.

"Any luck?" he asked.

"Nope," Puppy replied. "He's not going to let go of that bag for anything."

"We'll see about that…" Fangs said, adjusting the settings on the control panel. Alarms began to sound as the plane dived sharply.

The curtain separating the cockpit from the cabin was flung open. "What's going on?" demanded Clang, his terracotta-coloured eyes wide with terror. He was still clinging onto his precious rucksack.

"We've lost both engines!" Fangs cried. "Please abandon all personal belongings and collect your parachute from under your seat."

The golem screamed and fled back into the jet's cramped cabin – taking the rucksack with him.

"It was worth a try," said Fangs with a shrug. "Take the controls, Puppy. I'm going to show Clang the error of his ways." With that he raced through the curtain and disappeared.

Puppy switched to the pilot's seat. The ground was rushing up to meet her and the needle on the altimeter was spinning like the blade of a fan. She tugged at the control stick as hard as she could and managed to pull the nose of the plane up just before it slammed into the dense forest below. The jet skimmed the tops of the trees, shearing off a handful of high branches and giving a pair of hibernating squirrels an early wake-up call they would never forget. Then – slowly – the plane began to climb again.

1,000 feet … 3,000 feet … 6,000 feet…

In the cabin, Fangs watched Clang desperately trying to get into his parachute. The time for disguises and pretence was over.

"My name is Fangs Enigma," said Fangs. "I'm an MP1 agent. Now, hand over the rucksack."

Clang gripped the bag tighter than ever. "I can't," he croaked. "You don't know what my boss will do to me if I give it to you."

Fangs sneered. "You don't know what I'll do to you if you don't." The vampire rushed at him and the pair fell against the door, ripping it off its hinges. And then they were out of the plane and tumbling towards the ground.

Clang was still struggling with the parachute as Fangs lunged for him, streamlining his body so that he could catch up with the clay henchman.

The collision caused the hollow golem to ring like a bell: *CLANG!*

"Well, at least we know where you got your name from," said Fangs as he pulled the straps of the parachute over his shoulders.

Clang kicked his legs in the air, spinning himself away from Fangs. The vampire grabbed his cape. If he could press the button hidden in the lining, the cape would stiffen and he'd be able to fly after the hollow henchmen and catch him.

But Fangs wasn't wearing his cape. He was in his pilot's disguise – and the ground was approaching fast. Clang had got away.

Cursing under his breath, Fangs pulled the ripcord on his parachute … and the sky above him was filled with dozens of pairs of underpants.

Fangs stared in horror at the colourful boxer shorts. He hadn't grabbed the parachute at all – he'd taken Clang's rucksack! As pleased as he was to have finally retrieved the bag from his target, he knew his delight would be rather short-lived if he were to hit the ground at over 100 miles per hour. He heard a WHOOMPH! and looked down to see that Clang had opened the parachute.

Fangs tapped one of his two long front teeth with his tongue. It turned blue. "I'm going to need a lift," he said.

Puppy's voice replied via Fangs's other tooth. "Already on my way, boss!"

The plane swooped beneath Fangs, scooping him back through the door and into the cabin. As the plane levelled out, Fangs staggered into the cockpit and fell, exhausted, into the empty seat.

Puppy eyed the rucksack in his hands. "You caught up with Clang, then?"

Fangs pulled the one remaining pair of underpants from the bag. "Yep, but it was a *brief* encounter."

TOP SECRET

MP1 Mission File #5

Project: Wolf World

Report by: Agent Puppy Brown

Prime Minister Sir Hugh Jands held the pair of underpants up to the light. "What are these?" he asked.

Fangs Enigma, sitting with me at the opposite side of the desk, took a sip of his drink. "Is that a trick question, sir?"

Sir Hugh's moustache quivered. "No, it is not a trick question, Agent Enigma," he growled. "Our intelligence led us to believe that Clang was carrying something that could be a potential threat to this nation, if not the world – and you return with underpants."

"Then I suspect your intelligence was wrong, sir," said Fangs.

"We ARE the intelligence, Agent Enigma!" an angry voice gurgled. My laptop was sitting open on the prime minister's desk and the face of Phlem –

a swamp monster and the head of MP1 – glared at us from the screen. "We were the ones who sent you to find out what Clang was transporting. Are you suggesting I was incorrect to do that?"

"Not at all, sir," I said quickly. "But it's true – all Clang had with him were pants."

"And not just one pair," Fangs pointed out. "There were dozens of them."

Sir Hugh leaned across his desk. "And where are the rest of these underpants now?"

"They floated away in the wind, sir," said Fangs.

"And the suspect?"

"I'm afraid he floated away as well," I said. "He had a parachute."

"We have a search team combing the area for him as we speak, Sir Hugh," said Phlem from the computer.

The prime minister sat back in his chair again. He stared at the pants once more. "I just don't understand what's so terrible about these things."

"Well, they're not very flattering, sir," said Fangs.

"Don't play games, Agent Enigma," sneered Sir Hugh. "You know what I think? I think you're trying to cover up for the fact that you got the wrong bag. I think you snatched this chap's laundry by mistake, and you're too ashamed to admit it."

"Fangs definitely got the right bag, sir," I said. "Clang didn't let it out of his grasp from the moment he boarded the plane."

"Well, something has gone awry," said Sir Hugh, "as these pants clearly aren't a danger to our country. What do you have to say for yourself, Enigma?"

Fangs calmly took another sip of his drink. "You don't happen to have any blood to go with this milk, do you? It's rather bland without it."

Sir Hugh's face flushed purple. "I am the prime minister of Great Britain, Agent Enigma. Do you really think I'm likely to have a bottle of blood in my office?"

"On the contrary, sir," said Fangs. "I'd say you would be one of the few people who *could* demand a regular supply of blood. Your position of authority must stand for something."

"GET OUT!" Sir Hugh roared, hurling the pants at Fangs. "GET OUT RIGHT NOW!"

He wasn't the only one to lose his temper. "Enigma! Brown!" Phlem shouted. "My office – twenty minutes!" The screen went dead as the video link was severed. I grabbed my laptop and scurried out of the room behind Fangs.

"The man is a fool!" Fangs said as we stepped out into the afternoon sunshine. The door to 10 Downing Street slammed shut behind us. "It's not my fault Clang didn't have anything more dangerous than underpants with him. How would Sir Hugh like it if we'd turned up with a bomb?

I bet I'd get blood in my drink if I did that."

We made our way through the security gates that separated Downing Street from the rest of London and then turned in the direction of Parliament Square. It was early evening and all around us people were either on their way home from work or sightseeing. It was a very warm evening – the latest in what had been a heatwave in the UK. Ice-cream sales had gone through the roof, and one particular company, Furry Ices, was doing especially well. One of their vans was parked up outside Westminster Abbey. Fangs wanted to stop and get an ice cream, but the queue was round the block and Phlem would be angry if we kept him waiting any longer.

Once upon a time, people might have been a little freaked out to find a vampire or a werewolf in the street, but everything has changed since the supernatural equality laws were passed. Nowadays, spotting a skeleton or a witch in public is nothing to be surprised about, and there are even a couple of zombies in Sir Hugh Jands's government. The world has come a long way from the days of people attacking their spooky neighbours with pitchforks and flaming torches.

Some things haven't changed, however. Just like the human world, the supernatural one has its fair share of villains, and it's the job of Monster Protection, 1st Unit, aka MP1, to track them down and catch them.

"I don't get it," I admitted, dodging around a group of goblin tourists to catch up with Fangs. "If all Clang had with him was his laundry, why did he hang onto the bag so tightly?"

Before Fangs could reply, a young blonde woman approached us. She was with a huge troll who was clutching a map in his thick fingers. "Could you tell me the way to Trafalgar Square?" she asked, taking a big lick of the ice cream in her hand.

I pointed back down the street. "It's just a few minutes in that direction. Go past Downing Street, and you'll see Nelson's Column right ahead of you."

"That is very kind," the woman said with a smile. Then she raised her face to the sky. "Thank you-oooooow!" she howled and walked off.

I froze. The woman had howled at me. Was she being rude about me being a werewolf? There are still some humans around who don't like sharing the planet with supernatural beings. This woman didn't look like the type to ridicule me, though, especially as her boyfriend was a troll. I watched the pair disappear into the crowds, still poring over their map.

"What was that all about?" asked Fangs.

"I've no idea," I said. "But we'd better get a move on. We don't want to keep Phlem waiting to give us our telling-off."

Ahead of us, we could see the statue of Winston

24

Churchill, which hid the secret entrance to the underground monorail that would take us directly to MP1 headquarters. Fangs strode purposely towards it.

"Evening Standard!" a newspaper-seller called to us as we passed. "Interest rates at an all-time looooooooowwwwww!"

Fangs spun round to stare at the man. "What did you just say?"

The newspaper-seller lowered his face from the sky and looked at Fangs blankly. For a moment, the only sounds were the passing buses and the singsong melody of the ice-cream van.

"Tell me what you just said," ordered Fangs.

"It's the ... er... It's the headlines, guv. Interest rates are at an all-time low."

"But that's not how you said it before."

Then another howl rose up – this one came from a businessman on the opposite side of the street.

"Hooooooooowwwwllll!"

Then another – from the driver of a

passing car.

"Hoooowwwll!"

And a third – from a young schoolboy.

"Hooooowwwlll!"

"Come on," said Fangs. "We'd better get to HQ.

Something strange is going on."

A short monorail ride later and we were sitting opposite Phlem in his office.

"Look," Fangs said, "before we discuss Clang's underpants..."

"Quiet," Phlem said, his slimy fingers working the buttons of a TV remote control. "Take a look at this..." He switched on a news channel where the anchorman was already part way through a breaking story. "... first of many people in London mysteriously howling at the sky. And we can now go live to our correspondent, Barry Hutchison, in central London. Barry..."

The picture changed to show a reporter standing outside the Houses of Parliament. "Thank you, Simon. Members of the public are indeed

27

howling tonight but no one is quite sure why or how**OOOOOOOOOOOwwwwwlll...**"

The camera stayed on the reporter for a second. His face was turned up to the sky. Then there was a burst of static and the picture vanished.

"What could possibly be causing this?" said Fangs.

The TV hissed again and a new face filled the screen.

It was a werewolf!

"I am causing this." The creature grinned.

"His name is Lucien Claw," said Professor Hubert Cubit, the head of MP1's technical division.

Fangs and I stared up at a bank of screens mounted on the wall of his laboratory. Each one showed an image of the werewolf who had appeared on the TV in Phlem's office. He wore a sharp black suit, and had piercing yellow eyes.

"Show me his message again," said Fangs.

"Again? You've just watched it through twice."

"Just do it."

The professor shook his perfectly square head. Early on in life, he had realized that facts and information only ever come in square things. "Books, computers, filing cabinets – all square and all filled with knowledge," he told me during my first week of training. "Tennis balls, potatoes and scoops of ice cream – all round and hardly any knowledge in them at all."

Determined that he would also be stuffed with information, the young Hubert built a tight-fitting wooden box to wear like a hat at all times, so changing the shape of his head as it grew, from a useless sphere to a fact-filled square.

It is for this reason that Hubert is now known as "Cube". He earns his living as MP1's top brain box – literally. The rumour is that he still sleeps with his head in the frame, just in case the corners round out at night.

"OK," he said. "Here we go..."

Claw's face sprang to life on the TV screen.

"I am causing this," he said. "But I couldn't possibly say why – not without letting the *wolf* out of the bag." Claw began to laugh manically, his sharp teeth glinting in the light. Then the clip ended.

"How did he do it?" I asked. "That clip wasn't broadcast on national TV – just to us. But how did he break through the MP1 firewall and play it in Phlem's office?"

"With help from you and Agent Enigma, I'm afraid," Cube replied. He led us to a workbench, where Clang's rucksack was connected by wires to a laptop.

31

"The clue was in what Lucien Claw said about letting the *wolf* out of the *bag*," Cube added. "The bag is indeed the culprit here or, rather, its zip is. One side of it is a video receiver, while the other accepts audio signals. Fasten them together, and they work in perfect harmony to beam their combined signal to the nearest television or computer screen. It's extremely clever."

I sighed. "So we carried Claw's transmitter right into the heart of MP1 HQ."

"I'm afraid so, Agent Brown," said Cube. "And it only gets worse. A tiny wi-fi chip sewn into the base of the bag began to steal information from the MP1 computer database the moment you arrived."

"What kind of information?" I asked.

"The address of every vampire clan leader in Europe."

Fangs snarled. "Clang was nothing but bait. We were *supposed* to get that rucksack from him and bring it back here. Claw wanted us to know he was behind all those people howling and he wanted those addresses. But why?"

"I can help you find that out," said Cube, putting on a pair of square-framed glasses. "By reversing the polarity in the two receivers, I should be able to pinpoint the exact location of Claw's transmission."

"I don't understand it, boss," I said to Fangs while Cube worked. "We know how Claw was able to send his message – but it doesn't explain why all those people started howling."

"Could they all be werewolves, like you?" Fangs asked.

"I don't think so," I said. I'd only met a handful of other werewolves since I first transformed, but I've been able to recognize them straight away by their smell. A werewolf's nose is very sensitive, and the aroma of a fellow lycanthrope is as obvious as someone wearing a T-shirt that

33

reads "I Howl at the Full Moon". Today, I'd not smelled a thing, although I supposed that could have been down to me, not them. I'm not exactly a normal werewolf.

You probably know that werewolves only transform once a month, when there's a full moon in the sky. But that's not how it works 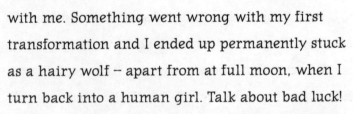 with me. Something went wrong with my first transformation and I ended up permanently stuck as a hairy wolf – apart from at full moon, when I turn back into a human girl. Talk about bad luck!

My school already had a couple of werewolves, but unless you were with them at full moon, you never saw them with their fur and claws. The opposite was true of me. Half the school thought it was hilarious, while the other half kept a wary distance. It wasn't easy for my mum and dad

34

either. They tried to make me look normal by covering up my fur with baggy jumpers, gloves and trousers, but it just looked like I'd raided a jumble sale. All in all, I was pretty miserable.

That all changed when I was recruited by MP1 and teamed up with Fangs Enigma – the world's greatest vampire spy (at least, that's what he calls himself). Since then, life has been a whirlwind of weapons-training, computer-hacking and secret assignments – and I love it!

"Right... This should do it," said Cube. "I've set the transmitters running backwards, so they should give us a fix on wherever Claw was when he sent us his message." He hit "Enter", but instead of a map reference, Lucien Claw himself appeared on the screen!

"Well, I wasn't expecting that to happen!" Cube exclaimed.

"You mean he can see us right now?" Fangs asked.

"I can also hear you, Agent Enigma," said Claw with a smile. "Please offer my congratulations to Professor Cubit. I knew he'd immediately try to reverse-engineer my receivers, effectively turning them into transmitters as well."

"Oh, so *that's* how he's doing it!" said Cube.

"Cut the chitchat, Claw," said Fangs. "Why are people howling?"

"Straight to the point." Claw beamed. "I like that." He paused to take a sip from a glass of red wine. "Do you know what else I like?"

"Don't tell me," said Fangs. "Long, romantic walks in the rain, and curling up in front of a log fire with a good book?"

Lucien Claw sneered. "No. I like the way things used to be, in the days when vampires and werewolves were mortal enemies. Two species prepared to fight to the brink of extinction. Before we were expected to put it all behind us and get along like old friends, so we would be accepted by the human race."

"The old days are gone," said Fangs. "Things are different now."

Claw let loose a throaty laugh. "That's where you're wrong, Agent Enigma. Some of us are ready to go back to the way life should be, with vampires and werewolves at one another's throats."

The camera pulled back to reveal two creatures with wolf-like fangs and sharp claws. Both of them were completely bald! They were ripping up chunks of raw meat and stuffing it into their

mouths. Could they be *werewolves*? Had they been in a fight with a vampire? Was that how they had lost their fur?

"With these creatures, we shall create a master race of werewolves, bred to despise vampires and everything they stand for," snarled Claw.

Another wolf, a female this time, threw more meat at the creatures. "And when our beautiful wolves are fully transformed, they will hunt down your kind, Enigma," she said. "Hunt you, and attack you until vampires have no choice but to bite back. The old way of life and death shall be restored."

I gasped. "You're planning to start a war between vampires and werewolves."

"Your little sidekick is correct," said Claw, "although I must admit to being rather disappointed by her willingness to spend time with a coffin-sleeper like you."

"Fangs is my friend," I cried.

"For now," said the female werewolf with a wicked smile.

"But soon, like all other supernatural beings, you will have to choose a side – vampires or werewolves," Claw added. He leaned closer to the camera. "You're a curious werewolf, Miss Brown," he said, taking another sip of his drink. "All teeth and fur, but without the full moon. I should like to get to know you better. Perhaps we can—"

Fangs cut the video link. "That's enough of him."

"He's a *werewolf*, boss," I said.

"Yes, I spotted that, too," said Fangs. "The clues were all there."

"No, I mean he's a werewolf like *me*," I said. "It's not full moon, but Claw and the wolves with him were fully transformed. They had their fangs and fur."

"But those two weird ones eating the meat looked like they'd shaved all their hair off," my boss pointed out.

"Maybe Claw could help me," I said. "If he can transform without the power of the moon, maybe he can show me how to become a normal werewolf. One who only changes once a month."

"Hang on," Fangs said, whipping off his sunglasses. "This guy's got people howling at the moon, remember?

40

And him and that female werewolf want the likes of me and you to tear each other limb from limb. This isn't someone you can go to for transformation tips, Puppy. We have to stop him."

"Of course," I said, trying not to sound disappointed. "I know that. So where do we start?"

"Were you able to trace Claw's position during the video call?" Fangs asked Cube.

Cube nodded, before handing over a piece of paper. "He's in Naples, Italy. Number Eighty Via Francesco Cilea, to be precise."

Fangs slid his sunglasses back on. "Then let's go knock on Claw's door..."

Fangs slowed the engines of the sleek white yacht and dropped anchor less than half a mile from the entrance to the port of Naples. Then he joined me on the boat's deck.

"Looks like we've got a clear run into the city from here," he said. He pulled a small bottle of

42

black pills from his pocket and popped
one into his mouth. Cube had invented
the tablets for him. He claimed
they contained the "essence of
midnight". In whatever way they
worked, they allowed my boss to
go out in daylight without being harmed.
It wouldn't be long until sunset, but the
fading light could still seriously injure a
vampire – or worse. Luckily, so far Fangs had
always been all right.

"Still no word on how Claw made all those
people howl boss," I said, looking at my laptop.

"Well, no matter how he did it," said Fangs,
"we're going to stop him."

"And I have just the equipment to help you
do it," said Cube, coming outside with a large
flight case.

I moved my laptop from the table on deck to
make room for Cube to put the case down and

43

open it. He took out
what appeared to be a
hardback book with
a silver cover. "I am
very proud of this."

"It's a book," said
Fangs.

"Yes, but it's not just *any* book..."

"Then what is it?" I asked.

Cube beamed. "It's the AnyBook."

"Hang on," said Fangs. "You just told us it wasn't
just any book."

"It isn't any book," Cube confirmed. "It's the
AnyBook."

Fangs pulled off his sunglasses and rubbed at
his eyes. "I'm getting a headache, and he's only on
the first gadget."

"I think I get it," I said. "You mean this book is
called the AnyBook."

"Precisely," said Cube. "Take a look at it."

"I don't want to worry you, professor," I said, flicking through it. "But all the pages are blank."

"Indeed they are," said Cube. "For now, at least... Inside the cover, you'll find a micro-thin keyboard. All you have to do is type in the title of the book you wish to read, and it is downloaded instantly from the archives at the British Library. Harry Potter, Scream Street, *Charlie and the Chocolate Factory* – whatever you want."

"But ... how is it going to help us stop a maniac from turning the world into one big werewolf-only club?" asked Fangs.

Cube waved a hand dismissively. "Oh, I'm sure you'll find a way! Next, we have this..." He took what looked like a kitchen cleaning sponge from the case and handed it to me. "Now, this isn't just *any* sponge—"

Fangs groaned. "Don't start that again."

Cube ignored the comment and continued, "This sponge is infused with the most powerful

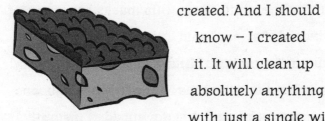

antibacterial detergent ever
created. And I should
know – I created
it. It will clean up
absolutely anything
with just a single wipe."

"Let's just hope Claw hasn't done the dishes by
the time we track him down," Fangs said dryly.

"There's no need to be sarcastic, Agent Enigma."

Fangs took the sponge and gave it a squeeze.
"Actually, I think there's every need."

"Is that all you've brought us?" I asked.

"Not quite, Miss Brown," Cube replied. "I have,
of course, left the best until last..." He opened the
case and took out a harmonica.

"What are we supposed
to do with that?" asked
Fangs. "Play Claw a
lullaby as he drifts
off to sleep?"

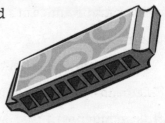

46

"Only if you are intent on suicide, Enigma," said Cube. "In the right hands, this musical instrument is a weapon."

"I can believe that," said Fangs. "I had to go to my niece's recorder recital a few months ago, and it was torture."

"How does it work?" I asked.

"It all depends on what tune you play on it," said Cube. "Play *Silent Night*, and the harmonica releases a dose of knock-out gas. Blast out a chorus of *Pop Goes the Weasel*, and you'll start the five-second countdown on a powerful explosive charge. I've emailed a list of which tunes activate which response to Puppy's laptop."

"OK," I said, slipping my laptop into its waterproof pouch. "Let's go. I presume we're swimming ashore?"

Fangs nodded and handed me a wetsuit. "Phlem has promised to have a vehicle waiting for us at the port."

47

Once we were suited up, Cube handed us our snorkelling equipment. "I think you'll find these will help you get into Naples undetected." Each mask and breathing tube was attached to a helmet with a plastic seagull bolted to the top. The end of a snorkel jutted out from the gull's beak. "The perfect camouflage!" Cube grinned.

And so Fangs and I swam from the yacht to the harbour in Naples, looking like a pair of seabirds bobbing along on the waves. We climbed onto the dock to find a rusting motorbike and sidecar waiting for us.

Fangs eyed the vehicle suspiciously. "That can't be for us," he said. "I'm sure Phlem would have ordered us something a little more ... comfortable."

I had to admit that my boss was right. MP1 kept cars on standby in every major city in the world, but they were usually up-to-date deluxe models and not as old and low-tech as this.

I examined the peeling paint on the sidecar and was surprised to find a state-of-the-art fingerprint scanner embedded in the rusty metal. There was only one organization that could have put that there...

"This is ours, boss," I said, pressing my thumb to the pressure pad. A green light flashed and the motorbike's engine spluttered into life. There were two safety helmets and two pairs of goggles on the floor of the sidecar. We put them on, and a few moments later we were chugging along in the morning traffic, clouds of black smoke erupting noisily from the bike's exhaust pipe.

"This isn't exactly how I pictured a visit to Italy," Fangs shouted over the roar of the engine.

"What do you mean?" I yelled back.

Fangs glanced at me. I could just about see his eyebrow arch upwards behind the thick lenses of his driving goggles. "I thought we'd end up cruising the streets in a sleek sports car. This is hardly likely to impress the girls."

I smiled. After settling back into the sidecar, I opened my laptop and launched the GPS software. "He's right, you know," I said, looking up from my computer screen.

"Who?" Fangs asked.

"Lucien Claw. You and I shouldn't really get along."

"Why? What have people been saying about me?"

I laughed. "Not like that. I mean as a vampire and a werewolf. Our races have always been enemies in the past, but look at us now – working together."

"I never went in for all that vampires versus werewolves nonsense, even before my kind came out of the coffin," said Fangs. "We are all the same deep down, no matter what species we are. I get on with just about anyone."

"Especially the pretty ones," I teased.

Fangs arched his eyebrow again. "I do have the odd weakness," he admitted. "Pretty girls... Garlic... Wooden stakes through the—"

WHIZZ! SMASH!

Right on cue, a pointed wooden stake zoomed past. We were under attack!

"It's Clang!" I cried.

Fangs spun round. An ice-cream van was speeding along the road behind us, its speakers blasting out a rendition of *Greensleeves*. Hanging out of the passenger window was Clang. He was reloading his crossbow with another wooden stake. If one of those was to hit my boss in the back, he'd be finished.

"Activate your cloak, Fangs," I cried.

"I can't," Fangs shouted. "I need both hands to drive."

I ducked underneath my boss and held the cape wide as I pressed a button hidden in the material. Once solid, Fangs's cloak would be able to withstand almost anything. The cloak stiffened just in time as—

WHIZZ!

Another wooden stake rocketed towards us. There was a deafening

CLUNK!

as the stake bounced harmlessly off the rigid material.

Of course, the cape only started at Fangs's shoulders. His head and neck were still vulnerable.

WHIZZ! CLUNK!

Another stake clipped the cloak and ricocheted away.

Fangs had the accelerator twisted round to full. The motorbike was travelling as fast as it was ever going to and it just wasn't fast enough. "Do we have anything we can fire back at him?" Fangs asked.

I shook my head. "Nothing."

WHIZZ! CLUNK!

"That one hit my shoulder," cried Fangs. "Think of something, Puppy!"

I made a quick mental inventory of everything we had with us. There wasn't much – just our bird-shaped scuba masks, and the AnyBook and harmonica that Cube had given us. The harmonica. Of course. That was it!

I whipped the musical instrument out of my utility belt and raised it to my lips–

WHIZZ! CLUNK!

"Puppy!" Fangs cried.

"Don't worry, boss. Clang's about to go out

with a *bang*!"

I began to play – which isn't easy with werewolf lips and enormous teeth.

"Half a pound of tuppenny rice,
Half a pound of treacle,
That's the way the money goes,
Pop goes the weasel."

I had five seconds before the harmonica exploded. One ... two ... three ... four...

I dropped the harmonica.

BOOM!

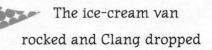

The ice-cream van rocked and Clang dropped his crossbow and fell back in his seat. His driver somehow managed to retain control of the vehicle. They were still coming after us!

"Clang's lost his bow, boss," I yelled, deactivating Fangs's cape. He would be able to drive faster without the cloak restricting his movements. "But we haven't lost them."

"I *wooden* worry," Fangs quipped. "We'll soon sort him out."

We drove on, opening up a gap between the vehicles. Clang gave a frustrated roar and pushed his driver out of the van. Then he slid into the driver's seat and floored the accelerator. He may not have had his crossbow, but he would still be able to do my boss some serious damage if he got close enough to stab him with one of the remaining stakes.

"I don't suppose you've got a better motorbike

tucked away in your utility belt by any chance?"
Fangs called to me.

"Not quite," I replied. "But I might be able to
give us a bit of a boost."

I pulled a grappling hook from my belt and
fired it at a road sign. The hook blasted forwards,
trailing a length of strong steel cable behind it.
It sailed around the sign's pole, and I pulled the
cable taut.

"Hold on tight!" I shouted. Then I looped my end
of the cable around the sidecar and pressed the
"Retract" button. The cable began to rewind and
the motorbike was dragged faster and faster along
the road. Behind us, Clang cried out again as we
sped away.

Fangs steered us to the curb. We snatched
up our equipment and then jumped out of the
motorbike. A crowd of tourists, attracted by the
hook stunt and Clang's angry shouts, had gathered
at the edge of the road.

"We need to lure Clang away from members of the public," I hissed. "We don't want anyone getting hurt by accident."

"There!" said Fangs, pointing at the entrance to a local bakery. "Fewer people inside."

We pushed our way through the crowd just as Clang brought his ice-cream van to a halt behind our motorbike. We had to make sure that he could see where we were headed, so he would follow us. The safety of the public remained our top priority.

Fangs was right. There weren't many people inside the bakery at this time of day. In fact, we were lucky the bakery was open at all. There were still enough customers to cause concern, however. Luckily, I quickly hit upon a solution and slammed my elbow against the fire alarm. It may not have been the most elegant of plans, but I was certain it would work – and quickly.

WAAAAAAH!

A loud, pulsing siren rang out and the bakery's staff and customers looked around in concern. "This is NOT a drill!" I yelled. "Please evacuate the building immediately!"

People began to rush out of the main entrance as Clang was coming in. The sight of a walking, talking piece of terracotta only gave them an extra reason to get out as quickly as they could. Soon, the place was empty, save for Fangs, Clang and me.

Clang spotted us and grinned. The good news was he had left his wooden stakes behind. The bad news was that he had snapped the pole off a sign post.

59

Fangs walked towards him bravely, despite his lack of weapon. "If it isn't the hollow henchman," he snarled. "Take a bit of advice from me – don't try to think on an *empty head*. The echo might scare you."

With a roar, Clang raised the pole and rushed at my boss. Fangs leapt out of the way at the last moment and the pole smashed through a counter stacked with cupcakes. Quick as a flash, Clang pulled the pole free and swung it sideways. He missed my boss by centimetres and destroyed a display case of pastries.

Fangs ran at Clang, knocking him into a cream tart and sending it to the floor with a **SPLAT!**

I pulled Fangs to his feet and dragged him through a doorway into the kitchen. After a snarl, Clang followed us.

My boss needed a weapon – but all I could find was a large wooden mixing spoon. It would have to do. I tossed it at my boss. "Catch!"

60

Fangs caught the spoon, just as Clang swung the pole around again. Somehow, Fangs managed to deflect the henchman's blow, while knocking the furious golem off balance at the same time.

Sensing that he now had the advantage, Fangs lunged at Clang with the spoon once ... twice ... three times. Each time the henchman managed to duck out of the way just in time. As my boss stepped in for a fourth time, Clang pressed his pole against my boss's chest and pushed as hard as he could. Luckily, the end wasn't sharp enough to pierce Fangs's skin, but he did fall backwards into a wedding cake. He slumped to the floor, covered in cream.

With the pole above his head, Clang gave a furious yell and lunged at my boss. Fangs raised his legs in the air. He waited until Clang's stomach was pressed against his feet, and then he thrust back with all his might.

Clang was thrown backwards through the air.

He smashed into an open fridge that was packed with eggs and exploded into a thousand pieces.

I ran over to Fangs, my feet squelching and slipping on the ruined cakes. "Are you OK, boss?" I asked, helping him to stand.

"I'm *eggs-cellent*," he said, grabbing a cloth to wipe cream from his sunglasses. "But he took some *beating!*"

We parked the motorbike and sidecar a few blocks away from the house Cube had identified as Claw's. As I unfastened my seatbelt, I noticed that Fangs was examining a handful of rolled-up pieces of paper. "What are they?" I asked.

"No idea," Fangs admitted. "I found them among the broken bits of Clang."

63

"They're scrolls," I said, taking a closer look. "It's how golems work. Whoever wants to control the golem just has to write down what they want it to do on one of these scrolls and pop it in the creature's mouth."

"That's what I call cheap labour," said Fangs.

I took a couple of the scrolls from Fangs and unrolled them. "'Kill Fangs Enigma, but bring me the werewolf alive,'" I read on one.

Fangs took that scroll back and tore it up. "I don't want anyone to accidentally swallow that one again."

"Why would Claw want to keep me alive?"

Fangs shrugged. "Maybe he's got a crush on you?"

"Trust me," I said, "The feeling is far from mutual."

Number 80, Via Francesco Cilea was a huge, gothic mansion with arched windows. We skirted around to the back, where I slipped a claw into the lock of one of the ground floor windows and twisted. There was a faint **CLICK!**, and I slid the window upwards.

We climbed inside. The house was silent. We crept from room to room, expecting to bump into Claw or one of his cronies at any second – but they were nowhere to be seen. We headed upstairs and into one of the bedrooms. Purple curtains ran along one wall, and in the centre of the room was a bed. A figure was lying beneath the duvet.

"Well, well," whispered Fangs. "Who's been sleeping in this bed?"

"Could it be Lucien Claw?" I asked.

"Only one way to find out." Fangs whipped back the duvet. "Wakey wakey, Claw, old chap! Time to greet the–"

But it wasn't Claw. It was a woman. There was something about her eyes that gave her identity away. This was the female werewolf we'd seen in the video – now back in human form. "Now there's

65

a sight to wake up to," she said. She sat up and kissed Fangs on the lips.

Fangs staggered backwards, his fingers rubbing at his mouth. He'd kissed a lot of girls in the time we'd been working together, but I'd never seen a kiss have an effect on him like that.

The woman climbed out of the bed. "My name is Scarlet Canis. I'm Lucien's business partner. You may recognize me from our video chat."

"Enigma," Fangs replied. "F-Fangs Enigma." He shook his head, as if he was trying to clear it. "We came here looking for Claw."

"He had to nip out," said Scarlet. "We knew it wouldn't take Professor Cubit long to track us down, but we were expecting you tomorrow." She yawned and made her way to a small bar in the corner of the room and began to pour out a glass

of milk. "Just as you like it, I believe – with a drop of human blood."

"Thank you," said Fangs with a smile.

He seemed to be more like himself again. "What time are you expecting Claw back?"

"He didn't say," said Scarlet, handing over Fangs's drink. "But you're welcome to wait. I'm sure I will be able to answer your questions. And I'm friendlier."

She kissed him again – causing Fangs to stagger once more. Milk slopped over the edge of his glass. Either this woman was the best kisser in the world, or there was something more sinister going on.

"Are you all right, boss?" I asked, hurrying over.

"He'll be fine," said a familiar voice.

Lucien Claw!

I spun round, expecting to find a werewolf standing behind us but, instead, it was a smartly dressed man with a goatee beard. This was Claw in his human form!

"Miss Canis seems to have this effect on men."

The woman smiled and began to reapply her blood-red lipstick.

"Where's s'other werewolvesss?" Fangs slurred. "There wasss sssome others here."

Now I really was concerned. Fangs seemed to be having difficulty focusing on Claw.

"I'll take that drink, boss," I said. "I think it may be drugged."

"How dare you, Miss Brown," Claw scolded. "I would never drug the drink of a guest!"

"Then answer his question," I said. "Where's the rest of your little gang? The two bald wolves?"

"They're in London." Scarlet Canis smiled. "Giving away our special ice cream – ice cream tainted with werewolf DNA."

I didn't like the sound of this. "Werewolf DNA?"

"Indeed," said Claw. "Our fellow wolves have been shaving off their fur so that it can be chopped into fine dust. This is then mixed with ice cream and devoured by gullible humans."

Scarlet Canis produced a small remote control from her pocket and pressed a button. A pair of curtains drew back to reveal a bank of TV screens. One by one, they flickered into life to show live feeds from CCTV cameras all over London. It was already night-time there.

"Some of the more susceptible people began to howl right away," she said. "Others required an extra dose. It's been such a lovely hot couple of days in London and our friends decided to give away lots of free ice cream..."

I remembered the van parked outside Westminster Abbey yesterday. No wonder the queue was so long! And here we were, in Naples, while the British public was being poisoned! I didn't want to let on to Claw and Canis that I was concerned, though, so I faked a yawn. "Are we going to watch more people howling?" I asked. "I hate repeats."

"Not *exactly*," Claw said. He pointed to a camera

which showed the half moon above the River Thames. "I advise you to keep an eye on the sky..."

Then something impossible happened. At least, I thought it was impossible. Scarlet pressed another button and the moon exploded with light. I was forced to cover my eyes to avoid being blinded and, when I looked back again, the moon was *full*!

I raised my paws up in front of my face, expecting my own transformation to have been triggered – but nothing happened. I ran to the window and stared up at the night sky. A quarter moon still hung over Naples – but in London, it was full.

"Impossible!" I gasped, turning back to the screens. "You can't change the shape of the moon, and you certainly can't do it over just one city."

"Oh, but we can." Lucien smirked. "And it appears to be having quite an effect..."

On the TV screens, people were falling over in

the street, clearly in agony. Men in business suits, taxi drivers, tourists – they were all transforming into werewolves. They writhed in pain as their limbs bent, their backs twisted and their noses stretched into snouts. The lack of audio only made their silent screams more distressing.

"Enjoying the show?" Scarlet asked.

I watched in horror as, one by one, these people sprouted fur and fangs and claws. Within minutes, the humans had gone. The streets of the capital were now populated entirely by werewolves! They raised their heads to howl at the full moon.

"I have the technology to redirect the sun's rays directly onto the moon, day or night," Lucien Claw boasted. "What's more, we can pinpoint the light of the full moon onto a single street, a whole city or even an entire continent! The vampires won't stand a chance against so many werewolves."

I turned away from the screens. "It's horrible! Stop it!"

"Sssssstop it!" Fangs slurred.

Claw sighed. "Miss Canis, if you would be so kind..."

Scarlet Canis grabbed Fangs by the collar and then spun him round. She kissed him again, longer and more passionately than before. When she pulled away, Fangs had red lipstick smeared all across his mouth. Of course! It wasn't the drink that was drugged – it was Scarlet Canis's lipstick!

 "Fangs," I said. "You have to stop kissing her!" But it was too late.

My boss's eyes rolled back in his head and he collapsed unconscious to the floor.

Canis pressed another button, and the full moon over London vanished. Once again, people fell to the ground, crying out in pain as they transformed back to their human forms.

"Now, why don't we have a little talk, Miss Brown?" Claw asked.

"I've got nothing to say to you."

"That is a shame. You see, I have a little proposal to make, werewolf to werewolf."

"You're not a werewolf! You're a monster!"

Claw laughed. "Perhaps – but you *are* a werewolf, and a rather special one at that. I almost couldn't believe my eyes when I first saw you during my little video chat with Fangs Enigma at MP1. Meeting you earlier would have saved us an awful lot of time and money..."

I was beginning to feel very uneasy. "Wh-what do you mean?"

"You're a werewolf that doesn't require a full moon to transform," said Claw. "Tell me – how do you do it?"

I glanced nervously at Fangs, who was still unconscious. "I ... I don't know. I just got stuck this way the first time I changed."

"Fascinating!" said Claw, running his fingers through the fur on my cheek. I batted his hand away. "Here's the thing," he continued. "Controlling the moon is impressive – but very expensive. And in addition to those costs, our friends have even started to demand payment in return for their fur."

I started to back away. "So? What does that have to do with me?"

Claw smiled in the half light. It wasn't pleasant. "So ... what if I infected our free ice cream with *your* fur instead of theirs? Your DNA would mean the population of the planet would stay *wolfed up* twenty-four hours a day. "

"No... No, you can't."

CLICK!

Scarlet Canis had clipped a dog collar around my throat.

"Oh yes we can!" snarled Claw, as he pulled a sack over my head. "You're our little doggy now."

"**Fangs?** Fangs, can you hear me?"

There was no reply — but then, in all honesty, I hadn't expected one. I'd been calling for help into my blue tooth almost constantly for hours, and no one had yet spoken back. I tapped the tooth with my tongue to turn it off.

I was in a crate, and the crate was on a plane. I was in total darkness, so I guessed I'd been put in the cargo hold. I wasn't going to get a complimentary packet of peanuts and the in-flight movie anyway. That was about all I knew. I didn't know for certain how much time had passed since Fangs had been knocked out, but my guess was at least two hours, maybe closer to four.

I'd been dragged, kicking and fighting, down the stairs in Claw's mansion and dumped in this box. I had quickly ripped my way out of the sack and was then able to see through a rectangular hole in one side of the box. I was taken to an airport – I had just been able to make out planes taxiing to and from the runway before I was loaded into one of them. We took off around half an hour later, although I had no idea where we were headed.

I hoped Fangs was OK. His lack of response to my blue-tooth calls worried me. The last time I'd

77

seen him, he'd been unconscious, knocked out by Scarlet Canis's kisses. What if he never woke up? Either way, I knew the wolves would want to keep Fangs and me as far apart as possible when they started shaving me. I shuddered at the prospect.

I tried again to break out of the crate. My laptop and utility belt had been taken from me, so I had to rely on brute force. I lay on my back and kicked against the crate again and again, as hard as I could. The walls didn't budge. In fact, they didn't feel or sound like wood. I began to suspect that the outside of the crate was lined with metal – perhaps lead. That would explain the communication problems. I could understand Fangs not replying if he was still unconscious – but my calls to MPI Headquarters were going unanswered as well. If the crate was covered with lead, then none of my wireless calls would be getting out. That meant I'd been talking to myself for hours.

My neck itched. I'd made several attempts to remove the collar that Scarlet had clipped around me, but it seemed to have a numerical combination on the lock and as I couldn't see it I had no way of cracking it.

Suddenly, the sound of the plane's engines changed. A motor was whirring somewhere over to my right. The pilot was lowering the landing gear. Wherever our destination, we were there. I felt a small bump as the aircraft landed and, after a few moments, we stopped. The engines died with a whine.

Pinpoints of light invaded the crate as the cargo hold was opened. The crate was lifted out and then placed on what I guessed must have been an open truck as some light was getting through the air holes. Perfect! That meant I'd be able to see out as we drove onto our next location, and I might even be able to pick up a few clues as to our location along the way.

The truck started up, and I pressed my eye to one of the holes to peer out. My neck was really itching now. In frustration, I slashed at the collar with my claws – but all I succeeded in doing was tearing the leather and exposing what felt like strips of metal. They gave me an idea...

I bit one of my claws, leaving it rough and jagged, like the blade of a saw and then used it to cut the leather. After a few minutes, I had managed to rip a section of the material away. I grasped one of the thin strips of metal inside the collar and pulled it free. Made from tin, it was flat and about thirty centimetres long. It wouldn't help me out of the crate, but that wasn't my plan...

I twisted one end of the metal strip around one of my fangs and then pushed the other end through an air hole. Then I tapped the

tooth with my tongue to operate the blue-
tooth communication system. A faint blue glow
reflected off the inside of my prison. If I'd done
this correctly, the metal strip should work as an
antenna, allowing the signal from my blue tooth
to escape its lead tomb.

"Fangs! It's me, Puppy. Can you hear me? Phlem!
Cube! Anyone at MP1 – are you receiving me?"

Silence.

My heart sank, and then I remembered that
this tooth could only broadcast my messages *out*
into the world. It was my other front fang that
picked up the replies, so even if Fangs, Phlem
or Cube were answering me, there was no way
I would be able to hear them. I briefly considered
pulling another strip of metal from my collar
and making a second antenna, before realizing
that I didn't have time – the truck could stop at
any moment. Instead I concentrated on getting
a message out.

"OK," I said. "I can't hear anyone responding, but I'm going to presume that someone can hear me and keep talking. I'm in a crate that's just been loaded onto a truck at a large airport. I don't know where the airport is, but the flight wasn't too long, so I'm guessing we're still in Europe. Wherever I am, it's dark outside. The only lights I can see are streetlights."

I pressed my eye to another hole in the crate and strained to see more of the outside world. "We've been driving for about fifteen minutes on some kind of major road – possibly a motorway.

There are signs beside the road, but we're moving too quickly for me to be able to read them." I sniffed at the air. "I can smell salt water. I think we must be close to the sea. And I can hear music in the distance. Folk music..."

The truck slowed. We were approaching the centre of a town. We stopped at a set of traffic lights and I was able to see a row of bars and restaurants through the hole in my box. Crowds of people were spilling out onto the pavements, chatting and drinking.

"It's a very busy place," I reported. "Lots of people are enjoying themselves and partying."

The truck pulled away from the main road then, and the revellers were lost from sight.

We drove on for another twenty minutes or so, and I continued to describe the route in the hope that either Fangs or Phlem were listening in. Eventually, we drove through an armed checkpoint and then a shuttered gateway into

what looked like a cave. The ground began to dip...
Perhaps we were heading underground. Then the
truck stopped.

This was obviously our final destination, so
I pulled the strip of metal back inside the crate,
detached it from my tooth and closed the line of
communication. I didn't want to get caught with
the home-made antenna, so I screwed the metal up
into a ball and did my best to hide it in a corner.

Then the crate was opened. Fluorescent light
flooded over me and I was forced to shield my eyes
against the glare. After spending so long in the
dark, I didn't want to risk blinding myself.

A man – possibly the truck driver – barked,
"Get out!" at me.

Muscles aching, I climbed shakily out of the
crate. Before jumping down from the truck, I ran
my paw over the outside of the box. I was right –
the entire outer surface was encased in lead.

"This way!" ordered the man. He pushed me

towards a huge, silver object floating on a vast
pool of water at one side of the cavern. I squinted
at it, because my eyes had still not quite adjusted
to the bright lights. Then I froze.

No! It couldn't be!

But it was.

In the middle of this huge stone chamber was
a nuclear submarine!

I stared at the submarine, trying to work out if
it was real or not. It certainly looked real. During
our time at MP1, Fangs and I have been trained
to recognize all kinds of military vehicles, and
this one looked like an old Russian Navy sub. The
words "Wolf One" had been painted along its hull
in bright red paint. Dozens of technicians in black
jumpsuits were busy working on different areas

86

of it. They seemed to be checking everything from the engines to the periscope.

"Move!" the truck driver grunted, giving me a shove.

He escorted me down a tunnel on the other side of the cavern. It led past room after room. Inside, dozens of white-suited men and women were making ice cream. So this was where they made the stuff. My throat was dry from the journey and I wished I could soothe it with some of the ice cream. I knew that would be a mistake, though, as it was full of werewolf fur. Yuck! Instead, I kept my head down and carried on walking.

We eventually came to a control room filled with computers and monitors. Here the workers were dressed in yellow jumpsuits. Seated in a chair on a raised platform in the centre of the room was Lucien Claw. Scarlet Canis was sat beside him.

"Miss Brown!" Claw exclaimed. "We've been looking forward to your arrival. Welcome to our secret dairy. A collection of natural caves we have excavated and added to over the past few months."

"Zip it, Claw!" I snapped. "Tell me what you've done with Fangs."

"Why, we've done nothing at all with him," Claw said. "He was in perfectly good shape when we left him in Italy." He turned to Scarlet. "Do you know how Agent Enigma is doing?"

"No," said Scarlet, "although he was a little *tied up* the last time I saw him."

"Of course," said Claw, pretending to remember. "Tied up and locked inside the attic of our house in Naples, if I recall. I don't think he'll be bothering us any time soon. Come, join us..." He gestured to an empty chair. "Spend some time with your fellow werewolves."

The truck driver pushed me forwards.

I didn't want to accept Claw's hospitality, but

I was exhausted after my long journey. I reluctantly slumped into the chair and accepted the glass of orange juice offered to me. I downed it in one.

One of the computer operators approached Claw and Canis with a clipboard. Whatever the technician had to show them, it wasn't good news. "No!" Claw barked. "I want to give free ice cream to the *whole* of Great Britain next!"

I quickly scanned the room. Amid the computers and control panels were the radar screens and depth monitors for the submarine. We had to find a way to stop ... *stop* ... them...

YAWN!

I suddenly realized how tired I was. In fact, I could barely keep my eyes open. I glanced at the clock on the nearest computer. It was 3.47 p.m. I'd been awake all night. I had to stay alert, no matter what. Had to stay ... alert ... no ... matter—

"Nuclear reactor powering up!"

Everything around me was shaking, and there was a roaring noise that sounded like an angry dragon with bad toothache. I jolted awake, convinced that it was the end of the world. I tried to move, only to find that I was strapped down to a padded seat. I was dressed in a bright red suit.

All around me were buttons and wires. Co-ordinates flickered on small screens in front of me.

I was on the bridge of the nuclear submarine!

There was a man, also in a red suit, sitting next to me. The visor of his helmet was down and I could see myself reflected in the glass. I thought back to everything I knew about submarine travel. This guy must be the helmsman – the officer who piloted the sub. It was then that I realized that we were both wearing *radiation* suits. That could only mean one thing – the nuclear reactor that powered this ship was not one hundred per cent safe!

How had I ended up here, dressed like this? I knew I'd been tired, but surely I would have woken up if someone had dressed me and carried me all the way on board a submarine...

Of course! The orange juice that Scarlet gave me must have been drugged.

I'd fallen for the oldest trick in the book!

A horrific thought occurred to me and I tore off one of my red gloves with my teeth to check if—

"Relax!" said a voice, making me jump. "You've still got your werewolf fur – for now." I craned my neck to discover that Lucien Claw and Scarlet Canis were sitting in the seats behind me. They were also dressed in radiation suits, although their helmet visors were raised.

"Where are you taking me?" I demanded.

"To our secret lair, of course!" Scarlet Canis beamed. "We could have taken your fur while you slept, but we have a little toy that we'd like to introduce you to when we arrive... The Shave-O-Matic! So much quicker than a regular razor and so much more painful too..."

I shuddered from head to toe. I didn't have time to dwell on what was waiting for me, though, as radiation symbols began to light up on the panels in front of me. The helmsman silently pointed at a red helmet on the console. I quickly put it on and

92

then lowered the visor, so that no one would see the fear in my eyes.

A voice crackled through the intercom. "Wolf One. Prepare rig for dive."

"The day is Friday. The time is seventeen hundred hours. Wolf One, prepared for dive," the helmsman replied. His voice sounded distorted through the speaker inside my helmet. "Power to reactor core."

"Power to reactor core."

"Levels in the bilge."

"Bilge levels at one point six and holding."

The helmsman gripped his controls. "Dive! Dive! Dive!"

The engines roared, and slowly the submarine begin to move. Green radar images started to sweep around in their circular screens, and the metal hull of the ship began to creak ominously. This was clearly a very old submarine. I crossed my claws that it would be able to handle the journey.

A voice crackled through the earphones in my helmet. "Wolf One, we have pressure in the boat."

"Copy that," said the helmsman. "Programming co-ordinates into main computer." He began to punch a series of commands into the control panel.

BEEP!

The pilot grabbed the controls. There was the tiniest of bumps as a message flashed up on the screen.

"Take her down," commanded the helmsman.

Then – suddenly – everything stopped. The noise, the vibration, the pressure – everything. All I could hear was the occasional **PING!** from the radar system. My ears popped as pressure built up around the submarine. We were definitely diving deeper now.

My thoughts were interrupted by another message. "Wolf One, we have a message for

Mr Claw and Miss Canis. Are they patched into the comms system?"

"We most certainly are." Lucien Claw's voice echoed in my ears. "What do you have to tell us?"

"Sir, we are getting reports that thousands of vampires are arriving in all parts of the United Kingdom."

"Excellent!" cried Canis. "The clans must have received our messages. How useful it was to get all their home addresses from the MPl database."

"What messages?" I asked, hoping I had a microphone as well as a speaker inside my helmet.

"Why, to our invitation to the big fight, of course," Claw said, proving that he could hear me. "There would be no point in creating millions of new werewolves if there were no vampires for them to hunt and slay, now, would there?"

95

"You're insane!" I cried.

"And you're ungrateful. Here we are, rescuing you from that disgusting vampire, Fangs Enigma, and giving you the opportunity to help spawn a new generation of wolves, and all you can do is complain," said Canis.

"Fangs is not disgusting!" I growled. "No matter what you might think about vampires, he is my friend, and he'll find a way to prevent you from starting this war."

"You're nothing but a vampire-loving traitor!" hissed Claw. "I shall enjoy shaving off your fur. It won't be long now. Look!" He reached between the seats to flick a switch on the control panel in front of me.

An image appeared on one of the screens and, through the murky water, I could just make out a shape looming into view. It was some kind of underwater base. The helmsman guided us closer and closer until—

96

CLUNK!

We docked alongside.

"Welcome to the Wolf's Lair," said Lucien Claw.

Lucien Claw took me by the arm and led me into the airlock that separated the submarine from the underwater lair. The door behind us closed.

HISS!

Once the air pressure had equalized, another door slid open – to reveal something I really hadn't expected to see. Standing just inside the doorway, with a loaded crossbow aimed directly at me, was Clang!

One of Claw's team had obviously glued him back together. Someone had clearly picked up some of the broken pieces of cookware from the bakery by accident, though, because the word "Flour" was printed along Clang's left cheek, and his nose had been replaced with the handle of a milk jug. He looked like a patchwork doll.

"Mr Clang has only one scroll inside him this time," said Claw. "He is under strict orders to guard you, and to kill you if necessary. In fact, it may be easier to take your fur if you aren't struggling..."

I glanced at the sharp, wooden stake loaded into Clang's crossbow and swallowed hard. I may not be a vampire, but that thing could do me some serious damage – especially if it was fired at close range.

Claw and Canis ushered us onto the main deck of the underwater base. There were two technicians there. I recognized them as the two werewolves I'd seen earlier – the ones who had provided their fur for Claw's ice cream – in human form. The ones I would be replacing.

"There's no point wasting time," Canis said to the helmsman. "Take her straight to the Shave-O-Matic. Meanwhile, Lucien and I will prepare for tonight's battle. Clang will join you when you're ready for the shaving to begin."

The helmsman nodded, and Claw and Canis left us.

"What's the matter?" I asked the helmsman. "Not got the guts to put me in that instrument of torture?"

He pushed me towards the large, silver box with doors standing at the far end of the deck. The word "Shave-o-Matic" was etched on its front. As we approached, a sensor beeped and the doors whooshed open to reveal a dozen whirring, metal arms inside, each one tipped with spinning blades.

WHOOSH! WHIRR! SNAP! WHIRR! WHOOSH! WHIRR!

"Look," I said, trying to pull away. "You don't have to do this, just because Lucien Claw told you to."

"I know," said the helmsman. "I won't."

I stared up at him in confusion. Hang on, he had to be tricking me.

"Really?" I asked out loud.

The helmsman raised his visor, and a familiar face smiled back at me. "Really," he said.

"Oh, Fangs!" I cried. "It's you!"

My boss hushed me as he glanced over his shoulder to check that Claw and Canis were still busy with their battle arrangements. "Don't let on who I am. Just take off your radiation suit and look unhappy."

I nodded, and he pretended to check settings on a keypad of the shaving machine.

"How did you find me?" I whispered, stepping out of my suit.

"Cube was able to pinpoint your location by tracking your blue tooth. We're beneath the lighthouse on the west pier at Dun Laoghaire in Ireland."

"Dun Laoghaire?"

Fangs nodded. "Claw and Canis are mixing their ice cream in the caves below one of Ireland's favourite holiday resorts. This undersea place must be their little hideaway. They wouldn't want to be anywhere near the ice-cream factory and its hairy treats, in case it's discovered."

"But I still don't understand," I said. "How did you get past Claw's guards? And how did you learn to pilot a nuclear sub?"

"With a little help from Cube and this..." Fangs beamed as he slid the AnyBook from inside his radiation suit. He opened its cover.

"*Nuclear Submarines for Dummies?*" I read.

"Don't knock it!" said Fangs. "It got us here, didn't it?"

Before I could comment further, Lucien Claw came stomping over. "I can't hear any shaving!" he bellowed. "Where's that werewolf fur?"

In one swift movement, Fangs had removed his helmet and slid on his sunglasses. "Puppy's fur is staying where it belongs," he said, turning to face the angry villain.

"Fangs Enigma!" Claw roared. "How did you get here?"

"I hitched a lift on a passing shark. How do you think?" Fangs climbed out of his red radiation suit.

"Clang!" Claw shouted. "Stop them!"

Clang came bounding over, his crossbow levelled at my boss.

"I like the new look," Fangs said to him. "Who's your designer?"

Clang snarled and pressed the tip of the stake against my boss's chest. "I've been looking forward to this, Enigma. It's your turn to get *smashed!*"

Fangs glanced down at the stake with a wry smile. "I do like a henchman who gets to the *point*," he quipped.

"Relax, Clang," said Lucien Claw. "You'll get your chance for revenge just as soon as tonight's festivities are complete."

Clang stepped back, but kept his weapon trained on Fangs's heart.

"Nice place you have here, Claw," said Fangs, peering out of the nearest window at a passing shoal of fish, "although I find the recycled air a little stale for my tastes. It dries the throat. Do you think I might have a drink?"

"Why not?' said Claw. He went to a drinks cabinet and poured Fangs a drink. "We could both do with a little refreshment while we watch the entertainment."

"There's going to be a show?" Fangs smiled.

"Indeed there is," said Claw, running his fingers over the Shave-o-Matic. "One with a *hair-raising finale*, especially for Miss Brown!" He

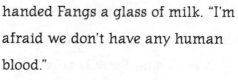 handed Fangs a glass of milk. "I'm afraid we don't have any human blood."

My boss sniffed at the white liquid. "That's OK. I wasn't planning to drink it, anyway." And he threw the milk over the control panel of the Shave-o-Matic.

HISS! BOOM!

There was a shower of sparks, and the whirring blades ground to a halt.

"Our machine!" Claw howled.

Fangs winked at me. "I thought you'd prefer to be *saved* than shaved!"

I sighed with relief. "Thanks, boss."

"You fool, Enigma," yelled Canis, rushing over. "Do you know how long it will take to get replacement parts sent down here?"

"Long enough for MPl to get the rogue vampire clans out of Britain, I should imagine. Your war is over before it even began."

"We will not be defeated!" Claw said. He turned to his technicians. "You two! Do we still have your fur loaded into one of the sub's missiles as a back-up?"

"Yes, sir."

"Then that will have to do for the first battle. Launch it now."

"At once, sir."

"The time for slow contamination by ice cream is over," Claw cried. "I will fire a fur-filled missile into the sky above Britain, where it will explode and shower the population with DNA-loaded dust. Once people breathe it in, they'll be howling before you can say 'lycanthrope'!"

"Perhaps," said Fangs. "But it won't be Puppy's unique DNA, and they'll still need a full moon in order to transform."

"You should already know that making a moon full is not a problem for us." Claw went over to one of the large control panels.

"But how?" I asked, remembering how the wolves had managed to create a full moon over London. "You never told us how you do it."

"A secret satellite is currently in orbit above

107

the earth," said Claw, pressing a button. "Actually, *satellite* is rather a grand term for what is, in reality, nothing more than a big mirror." On a video screen in front of us I could see a large satellite dish floating in space.

"Of course!" I gasped. "You reflect sunlight onto the moon ..."

"... and depending on the angle and focus of the mirror, you can direct that beam down to anywhere at all on earth," Fangs finished.

"Brilliant, isn't it?" said Canis. "Although it is a tad on the expensive side. Still, we won't need it after we began to harvest Miss Brown's rather special fur..."

"But if you just want to kill vampires, why not focus the sunlight directly onto the earth?" I asked, changing the subject quickly. "They'd all fry."

Fangs shifted uncomfortably. "Don't give them any ideas, Puppy."

"I admire your thinking, Miss Brown." Claw
smiled. "But cold-blooded murder isn't quite our
style. Besides, this way, we give the vampires a
fighting chance to survive. A very slim fighting
chance admittedly."

"You know, we can focus the light of the full
moon anywhere," said Canis. "Even all the way
down here, under water."

"What do you mean?" I asked.

"Well," said Claw, smiling wickedly, "we do
have to fill the time while
Londoners breathe
in the wolf DNA
somehow, and I have
to pay Agent Enigma
back for delaying us
getting your fur... So,

what say we have the first battle between
the vampires and the werewolves right here?"

Canis clapped her hands, excitedly.

Claw pushed a joystick forward. I watched on the computer monitor as the orbiting dish caught the light of the sun and then lit up like a firework. I had to shield my eyes against the single, powerful beam that bounced off the moon and down onto the earth below. It looked like a pure white laser beam slamming into the sea halfway between Britain and Ireland.

Then light shot in through the windows of the secret base.

Lucien Claw, Scarlet Canis and the two technicians fell to the floor, crying out in pain as their werewolf transformations began.

And so did I. Claw had triggered my transformation as well!

Every cell in my body exploded at the same second. My fur began to retract, leaving behind smooth, pale skin. My snout shrank, and my ears slid down from the top of my head. And my tail was getting smaller and melting into the base

of my spine. Blonde
pigtails flopped
down over
my ears, and
I looked down
to discover that
I was wearing
a yellow, checked
school dress.

"Wha–? Where
am I?" I groaned, my
head spinning. I could
remember the transformation, but nothing before
that. "Who are you people?"

Someone dressed in a smart shirt and long,
black cape crouched in front of me. He looked
familiar, but I couldn't place him. "Puppy," he said.
"It'll be OK."

"Puppy?" I repeated. I'd heard that name
before – but it wasn't mine. "No, you've got it

wrong. My name is Poppy." I clutched my dizzy head.

"OK, Poppy," said the stranger. He took my hand and squeezed it. "You're perfectly safe, just try to remain calm." He smiled, showing sharp teeth. Sharp teeth ... black cape. I started to feel very sick. This man was a ... a ... vampire!

"AAARRRGGGHHH!"

I screamed and pulled away from the vampire. Then I realized there were other creatures in the room as well – furry ones with pointed teeth and claws. They were ... WEREWOLVES!

This had to be a nightmare!

"AAAAAARRRRGGGGGHHHH!"

My name is Special Agent Fangs Enigma, and I was forced to take over the narration of the assignment at this point as my assistant, Agent Puppy Brown, had, well ... she'd changed. By all accounts, she became trapped as a werewolf during her first transformation, only changing back into a human at the full moon. Claw's full moon triggered her change on the submarine.

She hid behind a sofa in the werewolves' secret underwater lair, begging to wake up from this nightmare and crying like a little girl. Mind you, that might have been because she was a little girl.

How did I react to her transformation? Why, I jumped to my feet heroically and sneered at the werewolves. I could tell it had the desired effect. Claw and Canis shrank back in fear. They both gasped at the sight of my rugged manliness.

"Nobody upsets my friend," I snarled, fixing Claw with a steely glare. Then I sprang into action, because I'm just that kind of guy.

I snatched up a decanter of milk and hurled it at the joystick that controlled the orbiting mirror. It was a genius idea, and one which I'd already employed to destroy the Shave-o-Matic, so I knew it would work.

POW! FIZZ!

The jar smashed against the control panel, sparks fizzing as the milk short-circuited the controls inside. Unfortunately, the werewolves had set their systems out in a completely illogical order, and I hadn't hit the computer that controlled the mirror but the one responsible for the ballast tanks that kept the lair on the bottom of the sea. Shorting the controls had set them running in reverse! Gallons of sea water began to flood into the control room.

The water was freezing and took my breath away. Lucien, Scarlet and their two goons were splashing about in the rising water, doing the *doggy* paddle (ha!). Puppy – or Poppy, as she now preferred to call herself – clung to the back of the sofa, sobbing as the icy water rose around her.

I swam with all the elegance of a dolphin and the speed of an electric eel over to the two technicians and hauled their hairy faces above the surface of the water. "You two," I yelled. "Get in the cargo hold of the nuclear sub now, and I'll see that MP1 treats you fairly!"

They nodded eagerly at the offer – and why wouldn't they? Surrendering meant they didn't have to face the awesome power that was Fangs Enigma.

"You cowards!" Claw bellowed as the pair began to splash their way towards the air lock. "Clang! Kill Fangs Enigma now!"

I'd forgotten about Clang! No matter. He was no match for me. I pumped my strong arms and swam in a circle just in time to see the henchman aim his crossbow and fire. The wooden stake shot towards me. I was forced to execute an impressive backwards somersault to avoid its strike. I even took a moment to gulp down some of the milk that had floated out of the broken decanter in mid-spin.

Unfortunately, the stake ricocheted off one of the computer consoles and sped back towards me. It clipped my arm and cut a deep gash that I knew was going to need stitches. I didn't mind, though. Chicks dig scars, and this one would be a belter!

Clang's face fell as the stake continued on its flight path and struck him hard in the chest. The point did not pierce his tough terracotta hide, but the force of the impact was enough to slam him back against the wall of the lair.

CRASH!

He shattered into a thousand bits.

"You need to get yourself a better goon," I said, spinning round to make sure my quip wasn't lost on just anyone. "This one keeps going to *pieces*."

Claw obviously has no sense of humour because he swung out his fist and hit me on the jaw. Years of MP1 training has taught me how to deal with pain, so I wasn't actually hurt (although I *may* have yelped like a baby kitten just to fool him into thinking he'd done some damage).

The punch knocked me back into the water. I dived beneath the surface and then swam across the control room to surface beside Puppy, er ... I mean Poppy. The computer panels were beginning to spark and fizz as the water reached them.

Then Scarlet Canis managed to activate the emergency pumps and the sea water began to recede. Less than a minute later, we were all flat on our backs on the floor, soaking wet, but still alive.

"No more delays!" roared Claw. "The transformation of the British public starts now!" After dragging himself across to the banks of computers, he slammed a hand onto a big, red button.

A robotic voice rang out. "Missile launch activated. Launch in ninety seconds ... eighty-nine ... eighty-eight..."

I grabbed Puppy by the shoulders and forced her to look at me. "You have to listen carefully..."

"You have to listen carefully," the vampire said. "I know you can't recall much, but you must remember me. My name is Enigma. Fangs Enigma. I'm the good guy here."

"But you're a vampire!"

"And *you're* a werewolf. You just don't feel like yourself at the moment."

119

I stared down at my skinny arms. "I don't *look* like a werewolf."

"You'll change back," Fangs assured me. "As soon as the light of the moon is moved away from this undersea base, you'll be your old, hairy self again."

I shuddered. "And the other were-were-wolves, are they g-g-good guys too?" I stammered.

Fangs shook his head. "They're planning to hurt a lot of people, and I need your help to stop them."

"My help? But what can I do? I'm just a kid!"

"You're a secret agent," Fangs said with a smile. "And a computer genius, too. If anyone can stop that missile from launching, you can!"

Over the vampire's pleading came the sound of a computerized voice reading out a countdown. "Forty-eight ... forty-seven ... forty-six..."

"Me?" I said. It all sounded so bizarre, like I was trapped in some weird, scary dream. "What do I have to do?"

"Just get to the computers and find one that's still working. Then you need to stop— *GLARK!*"

Fangs's voice was cut off as the female werewolf reached over the sofa and wrapped her paws around his throat.

"Go!" Fangs croaked. "Go now!"

Shivering with a mixture of fear and the effects of the cold water, I crawled out from behind the sofa and looked around. Everything was in disarray and soaking wet. Bits of broken pottery covered the floor and all the furniture and paperwork had been overturned. Two of the werewolves had disappeared inside the submarine, so that just left the one called Claw and the one who was trying to strangle Fangs.

Except she wasn't trying to strangle him now ... she was trying to kiss him with her huge werewolf lips! A voice at the back of my mind told me

that this would be a very bad thing to happen –
but I couldn't work out why. Something to do with
her lipstick, I think...

"Fifty-seven ... fifty-six ... fifty-five..."

The floor lurched as the base shifted on the
seabed. I jumped at the nerve-shattering sound of
metal grinding against rock.

SCREEECH!

Suddenly the bright moonlight that had been
flooding the room disappeared.

"Scarlet!" yelled Claw. "I'll have to secure the
moorings. The water has damaged our position.
Keep our guests under control!" He climbed
a ladder that was bolted onto the wall and
disappeared through a hatch in the roof of the
submarine.

"Now, Pu-Poppy!" the vampire called Fangs
cried. He was still fighting to escape the clutches
of the female werewolf. "Get to the control panel!"

122

I was still very confused by what was happening, but Fangs had been kind to me, and I wanted to help him. I jumped to my feet and raced across the room to the nearest computer. Thankfully, it didn't seem to have been damaged by the water.

"Thirty-two ... thirty-one seconds to missile launch..."

I picked up a chair and sat down at the keyboard – but I had no idea what I should do next! I'd done a few computer classes at school, but that was just basic programming. My teacher hadn't explained how to stop a missile packed with werewolf fur! I was going to have to guess how to–

OW!

The ends of my fingers burst open and long, yellow claws slid out. I wanted to scream but – for some reason – I felt happy that this was happening. Maybe Fangs was right.

Maybe I really was a werewolf secret agent.
I scratched the fur on the back of my hands and
tried to concentrate on the computer in front of me.

Wait a minute! There was *fur* on the back of my
hands, and all up my arms! And it was starting to
spread across my face, as well. The weirdest thing
of all was that it felt pretty good!

And suddenly I knew how to operate the
computer. I tapped in a few keywords. If only I had
my own laptop, I'd be able to hack into
the system and—

My laptop! I remembered my MPl
laptop – and Cube. I remembered
Cube! My tail wagged happily
as memories flooded back.

The countdown to launch continued. "Twenty-
five ... twenty-four ... twenty-three..."

GRR! ARG!

Fangs was still wrestling with the werewolf,
even as she changed back into human form.

"Hold still, Enigma!" she cried. "It's time for a snog and a snooze!"

"Not if I wipe that smile off your face first," sneered Fangs. Then he pulled a kitchen sponge from his pocket – the one I remembered Cube giving to us – and wiped it hard across her mouth. Her lipstick disappeared, leaving her lips pale and free of anything dangerous.

And then Fangs kissed her. He kissed her long and hard and when he finally released her, her eyes rolled back in her head and she collapsed to the floor.

"She's out cold!" I exclaimed.

The corners of Fangs's mouth curled up into a smile. "She's not the only one who's good at kissing! I'll bring her round when we get back home."

"That's where you're wrong, Agent Enigma," snarled Claw, re-emerging through the hatch in the floor. He too had reverted to his human form. "Neither of you will be going home!"

I turned back to the computer. My claws
whizzed across the keyboard as I searched through
the list of computer commands, trying to find the
one that would abort the rocket.

"Nineteen ... eighteen ... seventeen..."

"Fangs!" I cried. "It's not working!"

"Get away from there!" Claw grabbed me by
the scruff of the neck and
pulled me off my chair.

"Leave her alone!"
Fangs growled.
He punched Claw
in the jaw.

Claw flew back
across the room
and crashed into
what was left of
Clang, grinding
the already broken
pottery pieces to dust.

There was no way anyone could glue the
henchman back together again this time.

Fangs helped me back into my chair. "Are you
OK?" he asked.

I nodded. "I'm fine – but I need to get back to
work." I glanced down at the nearest monitor.

Fangs grinned down at me. "Nice to have you
back with us!"

Suddenly, there was a roar and Claw
hurled himself at Fangs, knocking
him off his feet. The vampire
and werewolf fought – and
then Claw produced a
wooden stake from
his pocket and aimed
it at Fangs's throat.
He must have found
it among the rubble
when Fangs had
punched him!

"Fangs!" I cried, leaping from my chair and trying to snatch the stake from Claw. The sharp tip was already pressing against the skin of my boss's neck.

"Don't worry about me. Just stop the missile, Puppy!" Fangs croaked. "If the humans in Britain turn into werewolves, the vampires will attack them and start a war."

Fangs was right. Saving humankind must always be our priority. Reluctantly, I sat back in my seat and tapped in command after command desperately trying to find the one that would stop the missile launching. It wasn't easy to concentrate with the sound of Fangs struggling for his life behind me.

"Six ... five ... four..."

With a final stab at the "Enter" button, I heard the command:

"Missile launch aborted... Missile launch aborted..."

128

There was no time for a sigh of relief, though.
The people of Britain may be safe, but Fangs wasn't!

"And now, Agent Enigma, you die!" said Claw.
I turned to see him kneeling over my boss, the
wooden stake raised above his head, ready to
plunge it straight into Fangs's heart.

"Funny, really," said Fangs.

Claw paused, the stake still clutched in his
hands. "What is?"

"Stakes," Fangs replied. "They're the only thing that can kill vampires, you know. Although we can be seriously burned by garlic. I hate the stuff, myself. And of course, there's sunlight—"

"What are you prattling on about?" demanded Claw.

"But why garlic?" Fangs continued. "No one ever says, 'The zombies are coming! Quick, get some potatoes!' or 'We're being attacked by trolls. We need to throw bananas at them!' Strange, when you think about it."

Claw snarled. "You are SO annoying. I can't wait for you to die!"

But that wasn't going to happen. Fangs had

distracted Claw long enough for me to creep up behind him. With a snarl, I brought the AnyBook down on the back of his head.

Claw collapsed, unconscious, on top of my boss.

"I always said reading was good for you!" Fangs quipped.

Then he hugged me hard.

CASE CLOSED
SIGNED: Agent Puppy Brown

Friday 1954 hours: **Nuclear Submarine, Irish Sea**

Fangs Enigma tapped a series of commands into the navigation computer and prepared to guide the submarine back home. "This is Wolf One calling Her Majesty's Naval Base in Clyde," he said.

"This is HMNB Clyde. Come in, Wolf One."

"Good to hear you," said Fangs. "I believe my bosses at MP1 have arranged permission for us to dock there."

"They have indeed, Wolf One. You are cleared to arrive in your own time."

"Roger and out!"

Puppy Brown entered the bridge deck of the submarine and sat in the seat beside Fangs.

"How are our passengers?" the vampire asked.

"Tied up in the cargo bay and complaining loudly." Puppy grinned. She watched Fangs press a sequence of buttons. "Are you sure you can helm this thing without the help of the AnyBook?"

"I've got someone ready to talk me in…" Fangs flicked another switch and the computer screen lit up to show Cube, his square head fitting the frame perfectly.

"You can pilot a nuclear sub, professor?" Puppy asked in surprise.

"*Pilot* one?" said Cube. "I helped design these things. And I must say our Russian counterparts are very much looking forward to having this one returned to them."

Fangs adjusted a few more settings and spoke into his headset. "Set depth at three two eight feet. Speed at zero six knots."

"Zero six knots is perfect, Agent Enigma. You'll be home in no time, and you should be back within range of blue-tooth communication now."

Right on cue, one of Puppy's front teeth lit up and a familiar voice gurgled out of it. "Agent Brown, I hear you survived your transformation in tact."

"I did indeed, sir," said Puppy. "How are things where you are?"

"Couldn't be better," said Phlem. "The vampire clans have been escorted home, the werewolves' satellite has been disabled remotely, and Cube has whipped up an antidote for the werewolf DNA. By the next *real* full moon, the only creatures howling will be genuine werewolves."

"Speaking of werewolves…" Puppy began.

"We're way ahead of you, Agent Brown," said Phlem. "Claw's technicians have been rounded up, and we're working with the authorities in Dun Laoghaire to repair the damage Claw and Canis did to the West Pier. We'll have secure transport waiting for your prisoners as soon as you land. That just leaves the matter of the underwater base, the Wolf's Lair…"

"What about it, sir?"

"I wondered whether MP1 should take it over as a kind of retreat, a secret location for agents to recuperate after dangerous missions?"

Fangs glanced at the video monitor as the submerged base disappeared into the gloom behind us. "I don't know, sir," he said. "It's certainly secluded, but I don't think anyone will be able to have any fun there."

"And why not, Agent Enigma?"

Fangs whipped off his sunglasses and winked at Puppy. "It's a bit of a *dive* down here."

ABOUT THE AUTHOR

TOMMY DONBAVAND was born and brought up in Liverpool and has worked at numerous careers that have included clown, actor, theatre producer, children's entertainer, drama teacher, storyteller and writer. He is the author of the popular thirteen-book series Scream Street. His other books include *Zombie!*; *Wolf*; *Uniform*; and Doctor Who: *Shroud of Sorrow*. His non-fiction books for children and their parents, *Boredom Busters* and *Quick Fixes for Bored Kids*, have helped him to become a regular guest on radio stations around the UK and he also writes for a number of magazines, including *Creative Steps* and Scholastic's *Junior Education*.

Tommy lives in Lancashire with his family. He is a huge fan of all things Doctor Who, plays blues harmonica and makes a mean balloon poodle. He sees sleep as a waste of good writing time. You can find out more about Tommy and his books at his website: www.tommydonbavand.com Visit the Fangs website at: www.fangsvampirespy.co.uk

TEST YOUR SECRET-AGENT

Spot the Difference (There are eight to spot.)

SKILLS WITH THESE PUZZLES!

Wolf World Facts

How well do you know this book?
Answer these questions and find out!

1) What type of creature is Clang?

2) Name the three gadgets that Cube gives to Fangs and Puppy to help them complete this mission.

3) What is the name of Claw and Canis's submarine?

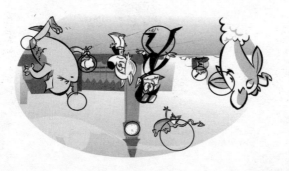

Wolf World Facts

A golem; the AnyBook, a kitchen sponge and a harmonica; Wolf One.

Answers

UNLOCK SECRET MISSION FILES!

Want to gain access to highly classified MP1 files?

Decode the word below and enter the answer at

WWW.FANGSVAMPIRESPY.CO.UK/MISSION5

Which Fangs character is this?

LCECAW UINL
